THIS WALKER BOOK BELONGS TO:

_____

_____

_____

The Search for the Perfect Child

For the cheeky little monkey, aka Zahra

First published 2006 by Walker Books Ltd, 87 Vauxhall Walk, London SE11 5HJ

This edition published 2007

10 9 8 7 6 5 4 3 2 1

© 2006 Jan Fearnley

The right of Jan Fearnley to be identified as author/illustrator of this work has been asserted by her in accordance with the Copyright, Designs and Patents Act 1988

This book has been typeset in Tapioca

Printed in Singapore

British Library Cataloguing in Publication Data: a catalogue record for this book is available from the British Library

ISBN 978-1-4063-0601-9

www.walkerbooks.co.uk

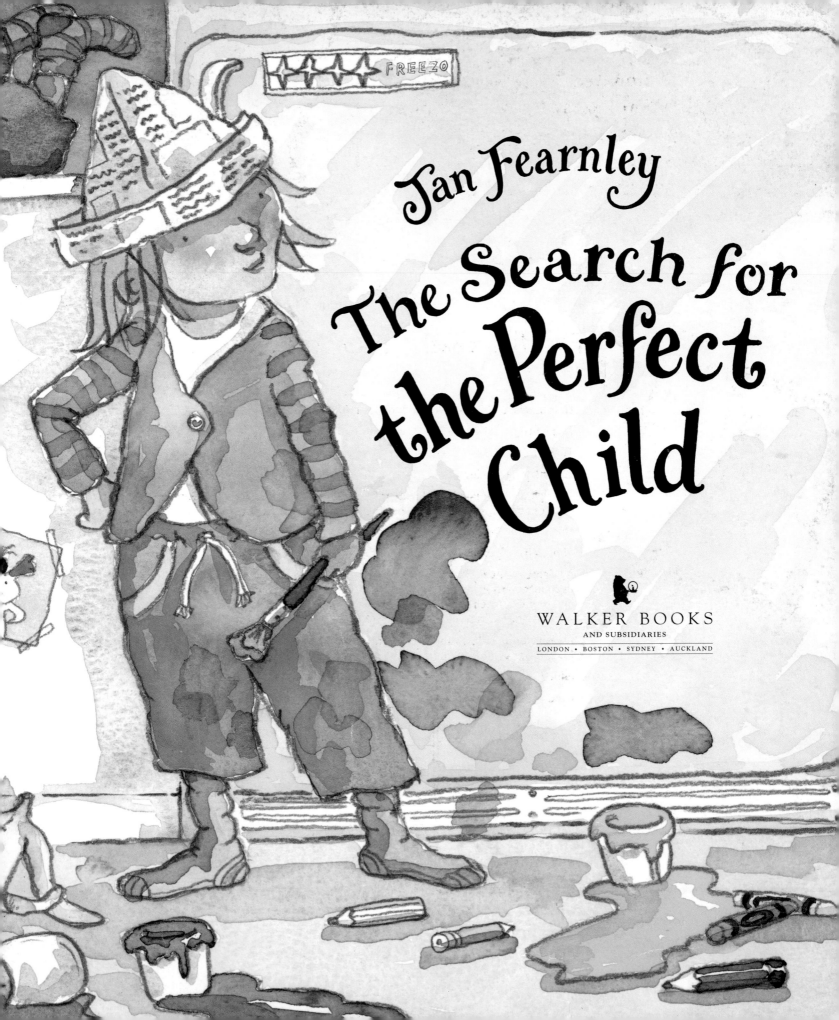

Jan Fearnley

The Search for the Perfect Child

WALKER BOOKS
AND SUBSIDIARIES
LONDON · BOSTON · SYDNEY · AUCKLAND

I'm Fido Fonteyn,
the **cleverest,**
sharpest,
coolest
dog detective in the whole world.

My eyes can spot
anything,
my nose can sniff out
everything,
even...

aliens,

pigs that fly ...

and gold at the end of the rainbow.

But now I face the hardest job of all – finding the **perfect** child!

People say there's no such thing,
but I'm going to sniff one out.

Hmmm.

What should I be
looking for?

What makes a
perfect child?

Some people say the **perfect** child is artistic ...

is kind to animals ...

and loves to grow things.

Others say the **perfect** child has style...

and is always happy
to help with the
chores.

The **perfect** child never complains about taking a bath ...

and has many different interests.

anything to do with toilets

bugs

flobble blobble nobble

silly words

spotting nose hairs at twenty paces

The perfect child
loves to monkey around ...

and, of course,
is **polite** and **well-spoken**
at all times.

Phew! It's not easy finding the **perfect** child.

Have you seen one?

Me too!
I've found **you,**

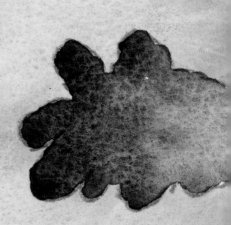

and **you** are the
perfect child.

WALKER BOOKS is the world's leading
independent publisher of children's books.
Working with the best authors and illustrators
we create books for all ages, from babies
to teenagers – books your child will
grow up with and always remember. So...

FOR THE BEST CHILDREN'S BOOKS,
LOOK FOR THE BEAR